I Am Helpful

A POSITIVE POWER STORY

by Suzy Capozzi
illustrated by Eren Unten

Random House New York

It is going to be
a great day.

Mom and Dad are bringing
my new baby sister
home today.
I can't wait!

I help Grandma get
the twins up.
All dressed.

Breakfast served.

Teeth brushed.

Ready for baby!
Grandma tells me
that I am helpful.

At last, they are home.
Baby Emily looks bigger
and cuter than she did
in the hospital!
Mom looks tired.
She looks so happy, too.

I know what to do.
I help Dad unpack.

While Mom rests,
Grandma shows me
how to hold Emily.
Sometimes we give Emily
a bottle.

I even help change
her diaper.
Pee-yew!

The days fly by.
Soon Grandma goes
home to Grandpa.
It's up to me to be
Mom and Dad's helper.
I've got this.

Sometimes it is
all about Emily.

Sometimes it is
all about the twins.
They can make
a lot of noise.

And then Emily
makes a lot of noise!
I know what to do.

We can go outside
to play.

Or we can stay inside
and read.
I am helpful.

Sometimes I want
it to be all about me.
Math can be tricky.
And Mom is really
good at it.

But Emily is teething.
So Mom has
her hands full.

Dad is busy, too.
He is putting
the twins to bed.

I figure it out.
Helping myself
is another way
to be helpful.

We take a trip to visit
Grandma and Grandpa.
It is Grandpa's birthday.

Emily is excited.

She is crawling everywhere.

Finally, it is
party time.
I help in the kitchen.

Then I set the table.

Now it is
time to eat!

I put Emily
in her high chair.
Then I set up her food.

There is so much
good food to eat!
Everyone is talking
and laughing.

Emily wants to join in.
She has something to say.
She blurts out a word.

It is her first word.
Everyone stops eating.
We look at Emily.
Emily looks at us.

She points to me
and says “June!”
She said my name!

I love my family.
It feels good
to help when I can.
I am helpful.

For Annie, whose compassion and support are limitless

—S.C.

To Wayne, for always helping

—E.U.

 Published in the United States by Random House Children's Books, a division of Penguin Random House LLC, New York. Originally published by Rodale Kids, an imprint of Random House Children's Books, a division of Penguin Random House LLC, New York, in 2018.

Step into Reading, Random House, and the Random House colophon are registered trademarks of Penguin Random House LLC.

Visit us on the Web!
rhcbooks.com

Educators and librarians, for a variety of teaching tools, visit us at RHTeachersLibrarians.com

Library of Congress Cataloging-in-Publication Data is available upon request.
ISBN 978-0-593-56493-6 (trade) — ISBN 978-0-593-56494-3 (lib. bdg.)
ISBN 978-0-593-56495-0 (ebook)

Printed in the United States of America
10 9 8 7 6 5 4 3 2 1

This book has been officially leveled by using the F&P Text Level Gradient™ Leveling System.